Hodder Toddler

This book belongs to:

....

To
YASMIN

MOUSE AND ELEPHANT
by An Vrombaut
British Library Cataloguing in Publication Data
A catalogue record of this book is available from the British Library.

ISBN 0 340 79945 5

Text copyright © An Vrombaut 1998

The right of An Vrombaut to be identified as the author and
illustrator of this work has been asserted by her in accordance
with the Copyright, Designs and Patents Act 1988

First edition published 1998
by Hodder Children's Books
a division of Hodder Headline Limited
338 Euston Road London NWI 3BH

This edition published 2001
10 9 8 7 6 5 4 3 2

Printed in Hong Kong

Mouse and Elephant

An Vrombaut

Hodder Children's Books

A division of Hodder Headline Limited

Mouse wants to
play a game with Elephant.

What can they play?
Can they . . .

. . . play
basketball?

Elephant
likes
basketball.

But Mouse
does not!

Can they . . .

. . . play football?

Mouse likes football.
But Elephant
does not!

Can they . . .

Elephant likes bouncing. But Mouse does not!

What can they play?
Can they . . .

. . . walk on the tightrope?
Mouse can (just about).
But Elephant cannot!

Elephant does not like ballooning.

Mouse does not feel like flying a kite.

Elephant really
does not
feel like
parachute
jumping!

It is no use.
Elephant is just
too big and
Mouse is just
too little.

Then Elephant has an idea!

Hammer, hammer!
Bang, crash, bang, ouch!

Elephant has made . . .

. . . a tricycle
that is just right . . .

. . . a mouse-and-elephant tricycle

. . . made for two!

Goodbye
Hodder Toddler